MW01107741

Funny Bone Readers

Making New Friends

Bunny and Bird are Best Friends

by Jeff Dinardo • illustrated by Jannie Ho

RED CHAIR
•PRESS•

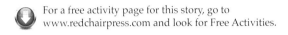
Bunny and Bird are Best Friends: Making New Friends

Publisher's Cataloging-In-Publication Data
(Prepared by The Donohue Group, Inc.)

Dinardo, Jeffrey.

Bunny and Bird are best friends : making new friends / by Jeff Dinardo ; illustrated by Jannie Ho.
p. : col. ill. ; cm. -- (Funny bone readers)
Summary: Two friends do everything together. But when Bird and her family go away, Bunny is
left all alone. This illustrated story helps young readers understand that even when a best friend
moves away, there are new friends to be made. Book features: Big Words and Big Questions.
Interest age level: 004-006.
ISBN: 978-1-939656-14-8 (lib. binding/hardcover)
ISBN: 978-1-939656-02-5 (pbk.)
ISBN: 978-1-939656-21-6 (ebook.)
1. Friendship--Juvenile fiction. 2. Moving, Household--Juvenile fiction. 3. Rabbits--Juvenile
fiction. 4. Birds--Juvenile fiction. 5. Friendship--Fiction. 6. Moving, Household--Fiction.
7. Rabbits--Fiction. 8. Birds--Fiction. I. Ho, Jannie. II. Title.
PZ7.D6115 Bu 2014

[E]   2013937166

This series first published by:
Red Chair Press LLC   PO Box 333   South Egremont, MA 01258-0333

Printed in the United States of America

1 2 3 4 5 18 17 16 15 14

Bunny and Bird were best friends.
They did everything together.

Bunny taught Bird to hop.
She was very good.

Bird taught Bunny to fly.
He was not very good.
But he had fun trying.

One day it got very cold.
The wind blew the leaves.
Bird got very sad.

Her family flew overhead.
"Time to go," they said.

"Winter is here," Bird said.
She flew into the air to join her family.
"I will miss you," she called to Bunny.

Bunny was all alone.

With Bird gone, Bunny was sad.
He had no one to play with.
Then he saw old Turtle.

"Will you play with me?" asked Bunny.

"I am too tired," said Turtle.
"I have to sleep until spring."
Turtle slowly walked away.

Bunny was alone again.

Snow began to fall from the sky.
Bunny felt it on his fur.
But he was nice and warm.

Then Bunny heard a noise.
Someone was crying behind a tree.

It was Squirrel.
"What is wrong?" asked Bunny.
"I am all alone," said Squirrel.

Bunny smiled. "Not anymore," he said.

Bunny and Squirrel played all winter.
They both loved the snow.

They had snowball fights and built forts.
They slid down hills on their bellies.
Bunny and Squirrel became best friends.

One day, winter finally ended.
The snow began to melt.
Flowers started to grow.
Bunny saw something in the sky.

It was Bird.
She and her family were home.
Bunny was happy to see her.

Bunny, Bird and Squirrel play together. Now they are all best friends!

Big Questions: Why did Bird's family go away? How did Bunny feel when Bird flew away? What did Bunny do to feel better?

Big Words:

spring: the season between winter and summer when plants bloom

taught: show someone how to do something

winter: the coldest season of the year